STACEY'S Remarkable BOOKS

BY
STACEY ABRAMS

ILLUSTRATED BY
KITT THOMAS

BALZER + BRAY
An Imprint of HarperCollinsPublishers

Balzer + Bray is an imprint of HarperCollins Publishers.

Stacey's Remarkable Books
Text copyright © 2022 by Stacey Abrams
Illustrations copyright © 2022 by Kitt Thomas
For information address HarperCollins Children's Books,
a division of HarperCollins Publishers, 195 Broadway, New York, NY 10007.
www.harpercollinschildrens.com

ISBN 978-0-06-327185-2

The artist used Procreate to create the digital illustrations for this book.
Typography Dana Fritts
Hand lettering by Laura Mock
22 23 24 25 26 PC 10 9 8 7 6 5 4 3 2 1
❖
First Edition

For Julie, who helped me be a better friend.
And, always, for Devin, Ayren, Riyan, Cameron, Faith,
and Jorden, who help me be a better person.
—S.A.

To my childhood best friend, Sheryl:
I'll never forget the exciting worlds
we created together.
—K.T.

It was recess—the best time of the day. Kids ran around the playground shouting and laughing, playing and jumping.

That is, everyone except for Stacey.

Instead of playing, Stacey lay beneath the big tree and read her book.

In books, she could pretend to be good at everything.
Like making new friends and trying new things.
When she read books, she could be anyone. A magician
or a superhero or a pirate sailing the high seas.

But in real life, she was just Stacey.

"Can I sit here too?"

Stacey looked up and saw Julie, the new kid.
They were both in Mrs. Blakeslee's class.

"Sure," Stacey said. "Want to read one of my books?"
Julie shook her head. "No, thanks."

"Do you like reading?" asked Stacey. "I love it."
"I do too," said Julie. "But I'm not very good at
reading in English yet."

Stacey thought for a moment and smiled.
"Today is your lucky day! Today is Thursday,

Adventure Day was her own special name
for the day the whole class visited the library.

Mrs. Blakeslee announced that it was time
to go back inside.

"Come on," Stacey said to Julie. "After math,
we'll be on our way."

Soon, the afternoon bell rang. Together, the class walked through the hallways to the library—the amazing room of books and magazines and computers and, best of all, stories.

When the class entered the library, Mr. McCormick, the librarian, greeted them with a smile. Then he repeated what he said every Thursday: "Welcome to the Library of Learning. Touch everything. Read anything. Find your new favorite book. And be kind."

Stacey showed Julie her favorite section of the library. Taking turns, they picked out a stack of books almost as tall as they were and walked carefully to a yellow reading table.

"Mr. McCormick says we can find answers to almost every problem in the library," Stacey said. "My mom and dad say reading well takes practice. Why don't we practice together?"

"At home, I read in my family's language," Julie explained.

Intrigued, Stacey asked, "What language does your family speak?"

"Vietnamese." Julie looked around the rows and rows of books that lined the library walls. "One day, though, I would like to read every story in here. I'd like to tell stories too."

Stacey understood—she had the same dream. To read every book ever written. To tell stupendous stories using extraordinary words. "Maybe if we read together, we can make our dreams come true."

Julie grinned. "I'd like that."

From then on, every Thursday, Stacey and Julie went on their own adventures. They hunted through the bookshelves to find tales they could read together. They giggled about an octopus who could play eight instruments.

A mystery about a hidden sock gave them the chills. With each book, they took turns sounding out the words. If Julie stumbled, Stacey would help.

One afternoon, Julie brought another
student, named Haddy, to their table.
Haddy's family had moved from
Gambia the year before.

"Do you want to read with us? We're starting a reading club," Stacey said. "In our new book, we're floating in space with astronauts and applesauce."

"The story is hay quá," said Julie. "That means 'so cool' in Vietnamese."

"Yes! I'd love to be in the club. Dama kontaan."
Haddy winked at Julie. "That means 'I am happy'
in Wolof."

Soon, they were adding new readers to their club.
They read at recess.

And at Julie's house.

By Haddy's pool.

In the park at Sam's birthday party.

Sam's family had moved from South Korea years before he was born. He showed everyone the book that Stacey had given him. "Gomawoyo," he said to her. "Thank you."
In Sam's new book, the reading club met a turtle who could predict the future.

With her friends, Stacey learned beautiful words in languages she had never heard before. And she got to know more kids in her class. The reading club got bigger and bigger, and the stories got better and better.

When the bell rang one Thursday, Stacey quickly got
in line. Genny, who sat on the other side of the class
from Stacey, came over.

"I'd like to join the reading club. I checked out an awesome
book about a dinosaur who learns to dance in the ballet."
Genny was very popular, but Stacey had never talked to
her. "I haven't read that one yet," Stacey said shyly.
"¡Vamos a reir mucho!" Genny exclaimed in Spanish.
"We're going to laugh a lot!"

More and more kids began to join the reading club,
like Vikal, whose family came from Indonesia.
Even kids from Ms. Bee's class. Each brought their
own words and different histories.

Mr. McCormick got permission for the reading club to stay after school. He brought them special books written about where each of them was from or in the languages they spoke.

One afternoon at recess, Julie and Stacey finished
another terrific story.
"Want to play kickball?" Julie asked.
Stacey shook her head. "No, thanks."
"Why not? They look like they're having fun."

"Because I'm not very good at games like that."
"Maybe if you played more, you could improve," Julie
teased her. "My friend Stacey told me it helps to practice."

Stacey stared at the kids running around. Her stomach wobbled, but this time she felt excitement instead of nervousness. If she tried, she could be out on the playground too. Spinning in circles and running like a cheetah. Laughing and having fun. Like her favorite characters in her favorite books.

Julie took Stacey's hand. "Come on, it will be an adventure!"

Stacey imagined kicking the ball so high, it would reach the sun.

"Let's go."

Author's Note

As a girl growing up in Gulfport, Mississippi, I spent a lot of time with books, diving into stories that felt exciting and fun and fantastical. Between their familiar pages, I could be as brave or as daring as I wished. Real life proved to be much tougher. I felt awkward and unsure of myself, like many kids do, and I was aware of the differences in race and class between me and some of my fellow students, without having the language to describe why it mattered.

Then I met one of my first friends, Julie Do. Her family moved to our hometown in the late 1970s from Vietnam. Like so many immigrants, Julie found herself on the outside. English was her second language, and she, too, felt isolated and alone. To me, few things are more tragic than language itself being a barrier to belonging. Knowing how hard being different could feel, I made it my mission to be a good friend to Julie. And she helped me too. When other kids would mock our differences, Julie gave me the courage to speak up. She accepted my weird sense of humor and helped me realize I didn't have to be someone else to be good at being me.

Almost ten years ago, I received an unexpected note from Julie. It read in part, "My Vietnamese name is Ha Do. A few days ago, I was at a social event, and we were asked to think of one individual who had made a difference in our life as a kid, and I thought of my dear friend, Stacey Abrams. We went to elementary school together in Gulfport. Being Asian in the South during that time was difficult, but Stacey showed me the true value of friendship. I remember how caring and funny she was, and, most of all, how much she loved the singer Prince." I treasure that note, and I keep it close.

In *Stacey's Remarkable Books*, I reimagined how Julie and I came to be friends—how we used words to connect us, stories to bind us. I take the liberty of bringing new friends back to that library where Julie and I spent hours talking about our favorite tales and our dreams of the future.

As the reading club grows in this story, my younger self also learns to face her fears and try new experiences beyond the tales in her favorite books. Each day, I try to live up to the expectations of young Stacey and young Julie. And I'm incredibly proud of grown-up Julie, who is now a special education and reading intervention teacher in a low-income community. I am delighted that our lives have come full circle.

To every child who finds these pages and dreams remarkable dreams, I wish you happy reading.

List of Stacey's Remarkable Books
(Feel free to add your own books too!)

Bilal Cooks Daal by Aisha Saeed, illustrated by Anoosha Syed

Crown by Derrick Barnes, illustrated by Gordon C. James

The Day You Begin by Jacqueline Woodson, illustrated by Rafael López

A Different Pond by Bao Phi, illustrated by Thi Bui

Drawn Together by Minh Lê, illustrated by Dan Santat

Dreamers by Yuyi Morales

Everybody in the Red Brick Building by Anne Wynter, illustrated by Oge Mora

Eyes That Kiss in the Corners by Joanna Ho, illustrated by Dung Ho

Festival of Colors by Kabir Sehgal and Surishtha Sehgal, illustrated by Vashti Harrison

Freedom Soup by Tami Charles, illustrated by Jacqueline Alcántara

Fry Bread: A Native American Family Story by Kevin Noble Maillard, illustrated by Juana Martinez-Neal

Going Down Home with Daddy by Kelly Starling Lyons, illustrated by Daniel Minter

Hair Twins by Raakhee Mirchandani, illustrated by Holly Hatam

I Am Enough by Grace Byers, illustrated by Keturah A. Bobo

I Dream of Popo by Livia Blackburne, illustrated by Julia Kuo

In My Mosque by M. O. Yuksel, illustrated by Hatem Aly

Julián Is a Mermaid by Jessica Love

Kamala and Maya's Big Idea by Meena Harris, illustrated by Ana Ramírez González

Like a Dandelion by Huy Voun Lee

Mama and Mommy and Me in the Middle by Nina LaCour, illustrated by Kaylani Juanita

My City Speaks by Darren Lebeuf, illustrated by Ashley Barron

My Papi Has a Motorcycle by Isabel Quintero, illustrated by Zeke Peña

The Ocean Calls by Tina Cho, illustrated by Jess X. Snow

Paletero Man by Lucky Diaz, illustrated by Micah Player

The Passover Guest by Susan Kusel, illustrated by Sean Rubin

Punky Aloha by Shar Tuiasoa

A Sky-Blue Bench by Bahram Rahman, illustrated by Peggy Collins

The Sound of Silence by Katrina Goldsaito, illustrated by Julie Kuo

Sulwe by Lupita Nyong'o, illustrated by Vashti Harrison

Thank You, Omu! by Oge Mora

Watercress by Andrea Wang, illustrated by Jason Chin

We Are Water Protectors by Carole Lindstrom, illustrated by Michaela Goade

When Aidan Became a Brother by Kyle Lukoff, illustrated by Kaylani Juanita

When Lola Visits by Michelle Sterling, illustrated by Aaron Asis